Dear Parents and Educators,

Welcome to Penguin Young Readers! As pa
know that each child develops at his or her
speech, critical thinking, and, of course, rec
Readers recognizes this fact. As a result, each Penguin Young Readers
book is assigned a traditional easy-to-read level (1–4) as well as a
Guided Reading Level (A–P). Both of these systems will help you choose
the right book for your child. Please refer to the back of each book
for specific leveling information. Penguin Young Readers features
esteemed authors and illustrators, stories about favorite characters,
fascinating nonfiction, and more!

Max & Ruby™: Ruby Writes a Story

LEVEL **2**

GUIDED
READING
LEVEL **I**

This book is perfect for a **Progressing Reader** who:
- can figure out unknown words by using picture and context clues;
- can recognize beginning, middle, and ending sounds;
- can make and confirm predictions about what will happen in the text; and
- can distinguish between fiction and nonfiction.

Here are some **activities** you can do during and after reading this book:
- Creative Writing: In this story, Ruby writes a story with Max's help. Now
  it's your turn to write a story! Start with the prompt "Once upon a time"
  and see where your story goes!
- Adding –ing to Words: One of the rules when adding –ing to words is,
  when a word ends with an –e, take off the –e and add –ing. With other
  words, you simply add the –ing ending to the root word. The following
  words are –ing words in this story: *crawling, going, finishing, making,
  playing, trying,* and *writing.* On a separate piece of paper, write down
  the root word for each of the words.

Remember, sharing the love of reading with a child is the best gift
you can give!

—Bonnie Bader, EdM
    Penguin Young Readers program

*Penguin Young Readers are leveled by independent reviewers applying the standards developed by Irene Fountas
and Gay Su Pinnell in *Matching Books to Readers: Using Leveled Books in Guided Reading*, Heinemann, 1999.

PENGUIN YOUNG READERS
Published by the Penguin Group
Penguin Group (USA) LLC, 375 Hudson Street, New York, New York 10014, USA

USA | Canada | UK | Ireland | Australia | New Zealand | India | South Africa | China

penguin.com
A Penguin Random House Company

ISBN 978-0-448-48746-5   10 9 8 7 6 5 4 3 2 1

Max & Ruby™

Ruby Writes a Story

Penguin Young Readers
An Imprint of Penguin Group (USA) LLC

Ruby is going to write a story.

"I have so many ideas!"

Ruby says.

Ruby has pencils, paper,

and a quiet place to write.

"I wonder how I should start

my story," Ruby says.

Ruby sits down to write.

"Once upon a time—"

she begins.

"Cowboy!" says Max.

"I'm sorry, Max," says Ruby.

"I don't have time to play

right now.

I'm writing a story.

Why don't you play cowboy

in your room?" Ruby says to Max.

"I need quiet to write my story."

Max goes to his room.

He puts on his cowboy belt.

He plays a song.

Ruby pours herself a drink.

"Writing makes me thirsty!"

she says.

"Once upon a time, there was

a . . . ," Ruby says as she writes.

"And then what?" she wonders.

"Cowboy!" yells Max.

Max plays a song.

"Max, I'm trying to write
a story," says Ruby.
"Let's find you something
quiet to play with."

Max plays cowboy with his

toy chicks in the living room.

In the kitchen,

Ruby sets out some cookies.

"Writing sure can

make you hungry!"

Ruby starts her story again.

"Once upon a time,

there was a—"

"Cowboy!" yells Max.

Max herds his toy chicks

through the kitchen.

"Max, if you want to play
cowboy, why don't you play
outside?" says Ruby.

Max plays outside

in his sandbox.

He uses a jump rope

to catch his toy!

Ruby starts her story again.

She sees Max's toy

crawling on the floor.

"Cowboy!" Max yells again.

Max catches his toy.

"Max," says Ruby. "I'm trying
to write a story, but you keep
playing around me.

First, you played music.

Then, you brought your toy

chicks through the kitchen.

And then you caught your toy.

You are making it hard for me

to think of what comes next in

my story.

I only got to start my story:

'Once upon a time,

there was a—'"

"Cowboy!" yells Max.

"Actually, that's a good idea!"

says Ruby.

"I know what my story is

going to be about!"

"Come on, Max.

You can help me write my

story!" says Ruby.

Ruby starts her story again:

"Once upon a time,

there was a cowboy,

and he said—"

"Yee-haw!" yells Max,

finishing the first line

of Ruby's story.